M000012869

Mrs. Bold, our teacher,
loves adventure.
She drives a rally car.

She climbs mountains.

She flies a hang-glider.

She flew the hang-glider
at the school picnic.
We drew pictures of her.

The next day,
Mrs. Bold came to school
with a broken arm.

11

12

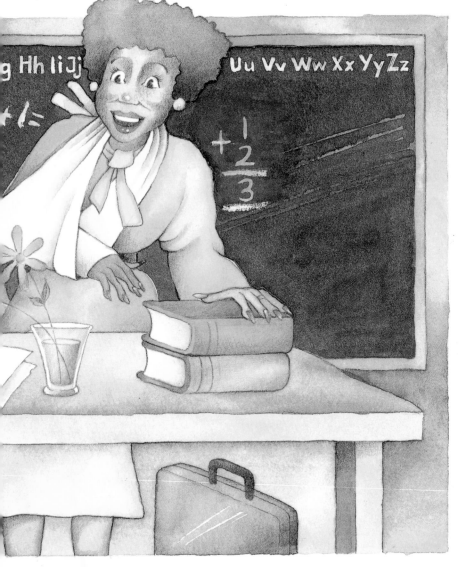

13

"Well," said Mrs. Bold,
"I was hanging your pictures
on the wall after school and...

15

I fell off the chair!"